And if you hypnotize me, will I not fart?

When he was done, Zaraband leaned back. He smiled a smile of total satisfaction. In a loud voice, he said, "When I snap my fingers twice you will forget you were ever hypnotized. But you will remember all of my instructions. And you will obey all I have told you."

"Yes, master," Bryan said.

Snap! Snap!

Bryan woke up.

He looked around, a little suspicious. Probably he had noticed that the whole room full of people was staring at him with their mouths open. Everyone wanted to know what was going to happen.

Bryan started down from the stage. Zaraband turned away. Everyone sat back in their seats, kind of disappointed.

Then Zaraband said, "So sorry to see you . . . *depart.*"

BLAAAT! Pop! Popopop! PA-TOOT! BLAAAAT!

Bryan erupted in a frenzy of farts!

Don't miss any of the books in

—the totally
GROSS
and hilariously funny
new series from Bantam Books!

#1 The Great Puke-off

#2 The Legend of Bigfart

#3 Mucus Mansion

#4 Garbage Time

#5 Dog Doo Afternoon

#6 To Wee or Not to Wee

Coming soon:

#7 Scab Pie

Visit Barf-O-Rama—the funniest gross site on the Internet—at:
http://www.bdd.com/barforama

TO WEE OR NOT TO WEE

BY
PAT POLLARI

BANTAM BOOKS
NEW YORK · TORONTO · LONDON · SYDNEY · AUCKLAND

RL 4, age 008-012

TO WEE OR NOT TO WEE
A Bantam Book / October 1996

Produced by Daniel Weiss Associates, Inc.
33 West 17th Street
New York, NY 10011.

ISBN: 0-553-48412-5

Published simultaneously in the United States and Canada

Bantam Books are published by Bantam Books, a division of Bantam
Doubleday Dell Publishing Group, Inc. Its trademark, consisting of the
words "Bantam Books" and the portrayal of a rooster, is Registered in U.S.
Patent and Trademark Office and in other countries. Marca Registrada.
Bantam Books, 1540 Broadway, New York, New York 10036.

PRINTED IN THE UNITED STATES OF AMERICA

OPM   0 9 8 7 6 5 4 3 2 1

To Michael

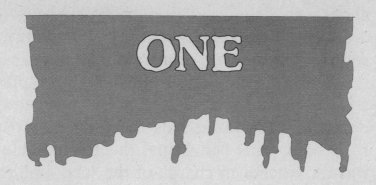

ONE

But soft! What whiff through yonder hinder breaks?

—Shakespew, Barf of Avon

"Hey, Alotsa Snotsa, what part are you trying out for? *Juliet?*" Bryan asked me.

"That's real funny, Bryan," I said. I grinned at the joke. Two jokes, actually. The one where he made fun of my name, which is really Alonzo. And the joke where he acted like maybe I would try out for a girl's part in the school play.

"Hah hah hah," I laughed.

Bryan is a very funny guy. He's also my best friend. But if you're going to hang around with someone as cool as Bryan, you have to get used to having him make jokes about you.

I mean, I guess my name *is* kind of funny. Alonzo. I'm the only Alonzo in school.

We were standing in the mostly empty school auditorium. There were maybe a dozen or two dozen kids there, more girls than boys. Plus Mr. Stipe, the teacher. He was the teacher in charge of the school play. The play was *Romeo and Juliet*.

It's by Shakespeare. I guess it's sort of famous. Even though it's a "love" play. You know, a romance.

"I'm going to be Romeo," Bryan said.

This surprised me. Bryan in a play? "I didn't think you were even interested in drama," I said.

"Drama?" He made a face. "Oh, you mean this play. You moron, of course I'm not interested in the play. It's just that it will get me out of English class and Ms. Holland hates me. She'll give me an F in English. But if I do this play, *this* will be my English grade. Ha hah! Pretty smart, huh?"

"Yeah. Really smart."

"Really smart. Reeeelly sma-art," Bryan said, making fun of the way I said it.

Which I guess was funny. Bryan thought so anyway. So I laughed along.

It's a good idea to laugh at Bryan's jokes. Bryan gets upset if you don't laugh at his jokes. And when he gets upset there's trouble.

Bryan is kind of big, in case you didn't guess that already. And he's tough. And mean. Kind of mean. But in a funny way.

"So. What are *you* doing here, Snotsa?" Bryan asked.

I shrugged. "Same as you. I was going to be in the play so I could get out of regular English."

"You zithead. That's so stupid. You already have, like, an A in English. Besides, who's ever going to give *you* a part?"

"I guess you're right," I said meekly. "I probably won't get it."

"I know why you want it," Bryan said. "It's because Kelly Armstrong is playing the part of Juliet and whoever is Romeo gets to kiss her."

"No way!" I yelled so loudly that half the other kids turned to stare.

Okay, look, maybe I did kind of like Kelly. But that wasn't the only reason I wanted to be in the play. Most of the reason, but not the only reason.

Then Bryan made a face, like something was the matter. He started patting his hinder. Nothing unusual for Bryan.

"Hey!" he said. "I think I have a hole in my jeans."

"A hole in your jeans?"

"Yeah. Take a look for me, will you?" He bent over and aimed his big reek cheeks at me.

I leaned over to look for the hole. I guess I should have known what to expect.

BLAAAT!

I was so close I felt the deadly wind of his buttnado!

"Aaaarrrgghh!" I cried.

"Hah hah hah hah! Oh, that was beautiful!" Bryan crowed. "I totally nailed you. Hah hah hah hah!"

I was still reeling from the morbific stench. Bryan is a guy who likes to eat things like sausage and cheese and potato salad. When he farts, the whole world knows about it.

"I can't *believe* you fell for that," Bryan said. "How come you're such an idiot?"

"I—I—d-don't know," I managed to gasp as I tried to suck in some unpolluted oxygen.

"It's a good thing you have me to look out for you," Bryan said. Then he grabbed me around the neck.

I tried to squirm free, but he had me good.

"Noogie! Noogie! Noogie!" Bryan yelled as he knuckled my head.

It hurt, but only a baby would yell or cry or whatever.

"Hey, you two! What's going on over there?" It was Mr. Stipe.

"Nothing," Bryan said.

"Well, it doesn't look like nothing," Mr. Stipe said. "Are you okay, Alonzo?"

Bryan let me up so I could say, "We're just messing around, Mr. Stipe."

"Well, we're not here to mess around," Mr. Stipe said. "We're here for the play try-outs. What part are you going to read for, Alonzo?"

I cringed. "Um . . . Romeo, I guess."

I looked at Bryan. He just shook his head like I was pathetic.

Which I was, I guess. I mean, that's what Bryan always says. And he's the coolest guy in school, so he would know.

"Good luck, Alonzo," Bryan said very sincerely. He even patted me on the back.

Which was nice, since he wanted to be Romeo too.

I practically crawled up on the stage. I was still gagging from Bryan's deadly fartillery. My hair was sticking up in the air from the noogie. But I felt better because he had said "good luck."

I crept onto the stage. Kelly Armstrong was already standing there, bathed in a soft glow of spotlights. Her blond hair seemed to form a halo around her head. She looked like an angel.

I stumbled crossing the stage. But Kelly smiled at me, and kind of shook her head. In a sympathetic way, you know? Like she was saying, It's okay, everyone stumbles sometimes.

I stood just a few feet away from her. I'd

never been that close to her before. She was beautiful up close.

I swallowed hard. I tried to remember my lines. I'd stayed up late memorizing them. And I said:

"Oh, she doth teach the torches to burn bright.

It seems she hangs upon the cheek of night

Like a rich jewel in Ethiop's ear;

Beauty too rich for use, for earth too dear!"

I had more lines, but then I realized people were laughing. People out in the audience, the other kids.

But some were not laughing. Instead they were going, "Eewwww, gross!"

I stopped, confused. Had I done something dumb?

Then I felt it. Something brushing my back.

I reached over my shoulder, and my fingers touched a sheet of paper. Someone had taped a piece of paper to my back.

I pulled it off and looked at it.

It was a Xerox copy of my face, all squished up. There was a big river of snot flowing from my nose.

I remembered the day. I'd had a bad cold. Bryan had grabbed my head and forced my face down on the Xerox machine. Then he had taken a copy of my smushed, snotty face.

Now that picture was on my back.

"Alotsa Snotsa!" Bryan crowed gleefully from the audience. "I hope Kelly doesn't mind kissing *that* face! Ha hah!"

TWO

O! 'Tis excellent to have a giant's strength, but it is tyrannous to use your friends as snot rags.

—Shakespew

Bryan got the part of Romeo.

When Kelly Armstrong spoke the immortal lines, "Romeo, Romeo, wherefore art thou Romeo?" it would be Bryan who answered. Not me.

I guess he was the best person for the part. Plus he just scared all the other guys away. Mr. Stipe was begging people to try out for the role. But after what Bryan did to me, the other guys figured maybe they didn't want to be in a play all that much.

Bryan scared everyone a little. Which was why I was lucky to be his friend.

Now, jump ahead in time. It's a week later, okay? And I'm waiting for the morning school bus as usual, when Bryan shows up.

"Hey, bird turd," he said. "You have that paper I need for history today?"

"What paper?" I asked.

"The one I told you to write for me. I have to hand it in today," he said. He stuck his hands on his hips and looked at me kind of sideways.

I swallowed. "Um . . . you didn't tell me to write a paper for you."

Bryan rolled his eyes. "You sit right in front of me in class," he said. "You know we were supposed to have papers today, right? About the War of 1812?"

"Well, yeah," I said.

Ah-CHOO!

Bryan sneezed. He gets hay fever some-times. But I'm not allowed to say anything about it. Bryan says only wieners have allergies.

"Look, if you knew we had papers due why didn't you do mine? You didn't expect *me* to write it, did you?" Bryan demanded. "I don't have time for some stupid war that probably happened back in the sixties or whatever."

I almost pointed out that the War of 1812 happened in 1812, duh. But Bryan doesn't like being corrected. "I guess I should have realized you wanted me to do a paper for you too," I said.

"Yeah, like ob-VEE-us."

Ah-CHOO!

Nose noodles!

I cringed. A heaping helping of fettucine al snotto had sprayed down and lay like a bad green mustache across his upper lip.

Should I say anything? Last time I told him he had a booger he yelled at me. He'd said, "No way. *You're* Alotsa Snotsa, not me."

But I didn't have to tell Bryan. I guess that load of warm snot on his lip was hard to miss. It was sure hard for me to miss. I mean, we're talking three, maybe four tablespoon-fuls of the green substance.

He was wearing so much green on his nose it could have been Saint Patrick's Day.

"Ewww, something on my lip," he muttered.

11

Then Bryan grabbed my shirttail. He yanked it up, and before I could do anything or say anything . . . He wiped that glistening sinus slime on my shirt!

"There you go, Alotsa Snotsa," he said, laughing. "Now you're even more than *Alotsa* Snotsa. You're a *Whole* Lotsa Snotsa."

For a second I wasn't sure whether I should scream or laugh. Laughing seemed safer.

"Hah hah hah. Good one," I said. I glanced down at my shirttail. The booger wad clung to it like glue. It was so heavy it actually pulled my shirt down on that side.

"You are *so* gross," Bryan said.

We both had a good laugh at that. I mean it was funny. Right? Besides, it meant he had kind of forgotten about the history paper.

I spotted the school bus about four blocks away. I wondered if maybe on the bus I could quickly write a paper for Bryan. Or else maybe I could just give him mine. Probably that would be best.

"You know what, Alonzo?" Bryan said. "This is too excellent a day for us to waste our time in school."

"Yeah. It is a nice day," I agreed nervously. A nice day aside from the fact that booger juice was soaking through my shirt.

"Let's bag school," Bryan said suddenly.

"Play hooky?"

"Hello!" He knocked hard on my skull. "Hello in there! Are you awake? What did I *just* say?"

"You said we should bag school."

He stopped knocking holes in my head. "Very good. I guess you're not a *total* zit brain. Come on. We're outta here."

He started walking away from the bus stop.

I hesitated. I really did not want to skip school. Not that I like school or whatever. But I was hoping I'd run into Kelly Armstrong— Juliet. I wanted to explain that the stupid picture she'd seen on my back was just one of Bryan's jokes.

I mean, I didn't want her to think I had done it myself, or whatever. Then she'd think I was an idiot. Of course, if I told her Bryan did it she'd probably think I was a spineless worm boy. Not everyone understands Bryan's sense of humor.

13

Which was worse? For her to think I was a moron or a wuss?

It was a dilemma.

"Come on, Snotsa!" Bryan yelled. "I don't want the bus driver to see me."

I started following him. "Where are we going?" I asked in my usual whining voice.

"Anywhere but school," he said.

Ah-CHOO!

Instant snot pudding!

I tried to hang back, to keep him away from my shirt. But now he had a two-nostril serving of goo laying on his lip.

Bryan grabbed me. He yanked at my shirt-tail.

"Arrrggghhh!" he yelled. "This shirttail has snot all over it!"

"Of course it does, you—"

But he just grinned. He spun me around and yanked up the back of my shirt.

SNORK! SNORK! SSNOOOORRK!

I swear he emptied a complete head full of boogaroni on my shirt. I felt like telling him to stop. I really did. But, well . . .

SNORK! SNOOOOORRRKKK!

"Ah, that's better," Bryan said. "Let's go."

I started walking down the side street.

"Hey," Bryan yelled. "Tuck in your shirt. I don't hang out with slobs. Tuck it in your pants."

"Hah, hah," I laughed, hoping it was a joke. "That's funny."

"It isn't funny at all," Bryan said harshly. "I mean it. You think a guy like me can be seen hanging with some loser who's covered with snot? Tuck it in."

At times like that I almost wondered if maybe . . . just maybe . . . Bryan wasn't really a very good friend, after all.

Nah, I told myself. Why would someone as cool as Bryan be hanging out with me if he wasn't my friend?

So, I grabbed the gooey, gloppy, viscous mess and jammed it in my pants.

It was most unpleasant.

THREE

Do you fire your flatus at me, sir?

—Shakespew

We went downtown to a video place that Bryan likes. We played video games for a while, with me losing every game.

Actually, I guess I could have won most of the games. Only, see, we have a special way of playing. Whenever it's Bryan's turn I have to stay totally quiet and not say anything to distract him. But when it's my turn he always makes jokes and gives me surprise noogie attacks and stuff.

So I always lose.

It probably isn't totally fair.

After a while Bryan said we should go to the movie down the street. But it turned out they were closed. Some guy was still stuck to the garbage on the floor from the day before. Then . . . I saw it.

"Hey, look," I said. "Across the street. It says Zaraband the Magnificent. Master Hypnotist! Special matinee show."

"I can read, pus-face," Bryan said. "Why would I want to go and see some stupid hypnotist guy? Only a moron like you would do that."

I shrugged. "I guess you're right. It's just that they hypnotize people and make them do dumb, humiliating stuff. I guess I figured—"

"Humiliation?" Bryan interrupted me. "Humiliation? We're there, man. Come on."

The theater was dark inside. Just like a movie theater. The show had already started. And there weren't all that many people.

In fact, I don't think there were more than fifty, scattered around the auditorium. We sat right up front.

Zaraband was already onstage. He was a kind of old guy. He had a pointy white beard and bushy black eyebrows, and he looked as if he hadn't been outside in the sun for a few years.

He wore a sort of black cape over a white shirt. There was a medal pinned to his cape. A big one. Like you'd get from one of those countries you can't pronounce.

He already had a person onstage with him. It was a woman.

"Your eyelids are growing heavy . . . heavy . . . ," Zaraband said to the woman. And he was doing this thing with his hands, where he would kind of wave them in front of the lady's face. "You can barely keep your eyes open . . . they begin to flutter . . . to droop. . . . You are becoming hypnotized!"

And the woman's eyelids did look like they were getting droopy and kind of sleepy.

In fact, I swear even my eyelids were feeling a little droopy.

"This is so bogus," Bryan said.

I think Zaraband may have overheard him. His gaze flickered toward us for just a second. But then he turned back to the woman.

"You will hear nothing but the sound of

my voice," Zaraband said. He kept waving his hands, even though the woman's eyes were totally closed now. "You will hear nothing but the sound of my voice. You will obey the sound of my voice. Whatever I tell you to do, you will do without any hesitation."

The woman stood there, looking like she was sleepwalking. Only she wasn't walking. But you know what I mean.

"Now, Ms. Younquist . . . I order you to open your eyes!"

The woman opened her eyes.

"Ppphhhhhhttt!" Bryan made a loud, rude noise.

My first worry was that he had snorked up another serving of mucustroni. But I guess his allergies were a little better inside, in the air-conditioning. So his noise-making was of the dry kind.

Again, though, Zaraband shot a look in our direction. His eyes narrowed. He looked kind of frightening, actually.

"Now, Ms. Younquist, I want you to become . . . a snake!"

To my total amazement, the woman dropped to the floor of the stage. She lay on her side and tried to slither around like . . . well, like a snake.

Zaraband stepped in front of her.

"Hisssss!" the woman said. She stuck her tongue in and out very fast. Like a snake. I was impressed. Kind of.

Bryan was not impressed at all. "Oh, man. Fake, fake, fake."

"It looks kind of real to me," I said.

"You swollen hemorrhoid! Give me a break. It's all just an act. That lady is just pretending. She probably works for that old fake hypnotist."

This time Zaraband definitely sent Bryan a dirty look. And a couple of the people in the audience whispered, "Be quiet!"

But another guy said, "Oh, the kid's right. This guy is a fake."

Zaraband looked down at the writhing snake-woman. "You are no longer a snake. You may stand up."

The woman stood right up, normal again.

"When I snap my fingers you will awaken,

and you will remember nothing that has happened."

He gave a loud snap. The woman jerked like you do when you suddenly wake up from a nap or whatever.

"Was I hypnotized?" the woman asked.

"There is some disagreement on that," Zaraband said. He turned to glare right at Bryan. "There's a young fellow in the audience who thinks it's all a fake. He does not believe that I possess a GREAT and MYSTICAL power!"

I shrank back in my seat. I'm sorry, but the guy gave me the willies. I've never known anyone who actually possessed any great or mystical powers, but this man seemed like he was the right type of person to be great and mystical.

He reminded me of my Uncle Dewayne. He always comes to our family get-togethers and tells us how there's a microchip implanted in his butt cheek by aliens.

Zaraband reminded me of him. You know. Creepy.

But Bryan wasn't bothered. He just laughed.

"Great and mystical powers, right. I'll show you something mystical." He leaned over in his seat and . . .

Pop! Pop! Popopop! BLAAT!

He fired a quick barrage of fartillery. Not his deadliest or loudest farts ever, but still you could hear them all the way to the back of the theater.

"Hah hah hah," Bryan laughed loudly. "Now, *there* was something mystical! What *was* that sound? *Where* did it come from? It's a *mystery*!"

He collapsed in giggles at his own amazing wit. And it *was* funny. Or at least it would have been, if Zaraband wasn't giving us a truly evil look.

"Oh, really?" Zaraband said in a silky, dangerous voice. "You think I'm a fake? You think I can't really hypnotize anyone I want?"

"You're a *total* fake," Bryan said. He stood up. "I'm outta here, old man."

Bryan started to walk away and naturally I fell into step behind him.

"Want to prove it?" Zaraband said.

Bryan hesitated. "What?"

23

"I asked if you wanted to prove it. Put my powers to the test. Step up here, rude little boy, and we'll see if I can hypnotize *you*."

"No way," Bryan said, snorting loudly.

"Scared?" Zaraband asked. He dragged the word out so it was like, "S-s-s-c-a-a-a-a-r-e-d?"

Well, what could Bryan do? The thing about being a bully is you can't back down or you'll look like a wuss.

"Okay, Zaraband the Magnificent," Bryan said. "Let's see you try."

FOUR

If you prick me, will I not bleed? If you tickle me, will I not laugh? And if you hypnotize me, will I not fart?

—Shakespew

Bryan climbed up on the stage. He was acting tough. You know, kind of swaggering like he wasn't impressed.

But Zaraband just stood there with this little smile on his face.

"Come along, young man," Zaraband said. "Step right up. Step right up. May we know your name?"

Bryan looked suspicious. But he couldn't look scared, so he said, "My name is Bryan."

25

Zaraband grinned again. It was not a happy grin. "Very good to meet you, Bryan," Zaraband said.

I got the feeling he was not sincere.

"I want you to look into my eyes, Bryan," Zaraband said.

Bryan kind of shook his head like Oh, this is so stupid, but he looked.

And then Zaraband started the thing with his hand. He waved it left and right. He waved it up and down. He made little circles. He did this shimmying movement, like a squid swimming.

"Look deep . . . deep into my eyes."

Bryan did.

"You will find that your eyes are growing sleepy."

"No they're not," Bryan said. But he blinked several times.

"Yes, your eyelids feel as if they are made of lead. They are so heavy. Soooooo heavy."

Bryan blinked a couple more times.

"Your eyelids are heavy. So heavy. You are sleepy. So tired. You would like to close your eyes. Yes, you may close your eyes."

And to my amazement, Bryan did close his eyes.

"You hear only the sound of my voice . . . ," Zaraband said.

"Only the sound of your voice . . . ," Bryan repeated.

All through this I was thinking, No way. This isn't real. Bryan is going to open his eyes and laugh at the old man.

But that didn't happen. Bryan just stood there while Zaraband the Magnificent waved his fingers back and forth and talked in a low, soothing voice.

"Now, Bryan, can you hear me?"

"Yes . . . I can . . . hear you."

"You must call me 'master,'" Zaraband said.

Okay, this would be the point when Bryan would open his eyes and—

"Yes, master," Bryan said.

Excuse me? I thought. Bryan calling someone "master?"

"You must do whatever I tell you to do, Bryan," the hypnotist said.

"Whatever . . . master . . . ,"

"I am going to give you a trigger word suggestion, Bryan. Whenever I say the word 'sun' you will become . . . a rooster! And you will crow like a rooster announcing dawn. Now, open your eyes."

Bryan's eyes flew open. He looked around and blinked. "See?" he said. "Nothing happened."

"I guess you are right," Zaraband said. "Maybe you would like to go back outside. Play in the . . . sun!"

" B b b b r r r r r a a a a a a w w w w k ! Bbbbbbrrrrraaaawwwwk! Errr a errr a Errrrrrrrr!"

The entire audience gasped.

I gasped.

Then, everyone laughed out loud.

Bryan didn't seem to even realize what he had done. He did not know he had just done a very good impression of a rooster. He thought everyone was laughing at the old man.

He swaggered over to the man and said, "See? You're a fake. Plus, your breath smells."

I guess Zaraband really didn't like the crack about his breath. Some people are very sensitive about different things, I guess. Zaraband snapped his fingers. Instantly Bryan fell back into a trance.

"You will no longer be a rooster," Zaraband said. His voice was harsh. He was annoyed. Definitely annoyed. "A rooster is too easy," he hissed. "I'm going to whisper a little something in your ear, you obnoxious brat. I'll give you some trigger words to remember, and you'll regret ever messing with me!"

Zaraband leaned close to Bryan's ear.

The entire audience leaned forward. Everyone was on the edge of their seats. But no one could hear what the hypnotist was saying.

Except Bryan, of course.

When he was done, Zaraband leaned back. He smiled a smile of total satisfaction. In a louder voice, he said, "When I snap my fingers twice you will forget you were ever hypnotized. But you will remember all of my instructions. And you will obey all I have told you."

"Yes, master," Bryan said.

Snap! Snap!

Bryan woke up.

He looked around, a little suspicious. Probably he had noticed that the whole roomful of people was staring at him with open mouths. Everyone wanted to know what was going to happen.

"So, I guess I proved what a fake you are," Bryan said to Zaraband.

"Absolutely," Zaraband said. "You were *totally* correct."

Bryan started down from the stage. Zaraband turned away. Everyone sat back in their seats, kind of disappointed.

Then Zaraband turned back around. He looked down at Bryan who was swaggering toward the exit.

Then Zaraband said, "So sorry to see you . . . *depart.*"

BLAAAT! Pop! Popopop! PA-TOOT! BLAAAAT!

Bryan erupted in a frenzy of farts!

Everyone turned to stare.

BLAAAAT!

"Ewwwww, get out of here, fart boy!" someone yelled.

Bryan clenched his fists like he was going to pound him. But before he could do anything . . .

BLAAAAAT! Poot Poot Poot Pa-TOOOOT!

I had never before witnessed such mighty farts.

Bryan looked a little sick. I stared at him in surprise.

"What are you staring at, nerd?" he demanded. He grabbed me by the arm and dragged me away toward the exit.

"Yes, *depart!*" Zaraband cried gleefully.

BLAAAAAAAAAAAT!

The power of that last fart was so great it seemed to push us toward the exit.

We escaped at last, followed by gales of derisive laughter.

Plus a few gagging noises from those who'd been seated within whiff distance of Bryan's under thunder.

FIVE

But, soft! Methinks I scent the morbific air.
                                        —Shakespew

As soon as we were outside, Bryan grabbed me by the collar. He pulled my face very close to his. His eyes were bulging. His cheeks had turned bright red.

"That never happened," he said. "You got me, Alonzo? That *never* happened."

"What are you—"

He tightened his grip till I could barely breathe. "You're not listening. We were never here. And this never happened. You tell anyone and you'll be dead. I'll stomp you. I'll turn you into hamburger. Got me?"

I nodded my head.

Bryan let me go and stomped away.

I think I was too shocked to be upset or anything. It was weird. Bryan has never been embarrassed by anything before. I mean, he farts all the time. He likes to cut big loud ones that make people turn around and stare.

So why was this any different?

I couldn't figure it out. At least not then.

I didn't see Bryan again till Monday at the bus stop.

He seemed to be back to normal. In Bryan's case "normal" does not necessarily mean "good."

"Hey, Alotsa Snotsa," he yelled when I got close. He stopped and stared at me. "Do you have my homework done?"

I nodded. "All except the science project. I can't do that—"

"What do you mean you can't do the science project?" Bryan demanded. "Do you expect *me* to do it? I have to memorize all that stuff for the play. Do you know how hard that is? I don't have time for stupid homework."

"I guess that's true," I said humbly.

"I mean, if you had gotten the part I'd be helping you out, right?"

The bus came and we climbed on board. Kelly Armstrong was sitting there with one of her friends, Jenny.

I kind of halfway smiled at Kelly. She kind of halfway smiled back.

"Hey, Kelly," Bryan yelled. "Are you practicing up for the big moment?"

"What are you talking about?" Kelly asked.

Bryan leered. "You know what I'm talking about. The big kiss."

Kelly got a slightly sick look on her face. "Oh, right."

"You must be the luckiest girl in school," Bryan said. "If they'd known I was going to be Romeo, probably every girl would have tried out."

Kelly rolled her eyes. "Could you possibly be any more conceited, Bryan?"

"Hey, why wouldn't I be conceited? I mean, look at me."

"I'd rather look at you leave," Kelly said.

"Go sit down. Get lost. Depart."

BLAAAAAAT!

"Excuse *you!*" Kelly said. She started to wave her hand in front of her face.

But Bryan was just starting.

Pa-TOOOOT! Pop pop pop pop BLAA-AAAAT!

"Aaarrggh!" someone yelled.

"The stench! It's awful!"

Kelly jumped up out of her seat and tried to run. But then, Bryan fired the single biggest flatus anyone had ever seen. Or smelled.

It started off slow, as a squeezer.

Ppppffffffffffff. . .

Then, it went multipopper.

Pop pop pop POPOPOPOPOP pop POP-OPOPOP!

And then, without warning . . .

KA-BLOOOOOOOOOM!

It happened so suddenly! There was no warning. NO WARNING!

Bryan was blown forward, like someone had shoved him. He landed right across Kelly.

My ears popped from the explosion. People's hair blew wildly in the deadly butt wind.

Kelly tried to shove Bryan off her, but then the wave of stench rolled over them both.

Kelly's eyes fluttered. She seemed to be going into a kind of fit, jerking and heaving and twitching.

Then, the wave of stench wafted back over to me.

There are no words for the putrid horror of that stench. It was heinous! It was most regrettable!

It was . . . morbific!

"Open the windows!" someone screamed.

"Save us!"

"I want my mommy!"

Wham! Wham! Wham! Windows were dropped open all along the bus. Sweet, fresh air blew in.

Kelly's face stopped twitching. Now, instead she just made a face, and shoved Bryan away with all her might. He fell to the floor of the bus.

He looked up at me with a horrified expression. It was sheer terror. I knew he needed me to save him. But before I could do or say anything to help, Bryan yelled, "Alonzo! Stop farting like that! You're making us all sick!"

I froze.

One by one, every face on the bus turned to stare at me.

"But . . . but . . . but . . . ," I said.

"Hey, we've heard enough from your *butt*," Bryan said.

That made everyone laugh—even the kids who were hanging halfway out of the windows to get air.

Wave after wave of laughter rippled through the busload of kids. They pointed at me. Some even threw things at me.

My face was burning with embarrassment and shame. But with Bryan glaring at me what could I say?

I shrugged. "Sorry," I said.

SIX

Double, double, toil and trouble, fire burn and bladder bubble.

—Shakespew

Now, you're probably wondering why I didn't figure out what was going on with Bryan.

But you have to remember, it was Monday morning. The thing with Zaraband had been on Friday. I wasn't connecting things. I mean, give me a break. I had school and parents to deal with. I'm not one of the Hardy Boys. I'm not some junior detective.

But two days later something happened that began to clear it up for me.

We were in science class. I had finally done Bryan's science project for him: It was this thing with a computer chip and arrows showing how it worked and all.

It was a pretty good science project. But he didn't like it.

"It's dweeb central," he sneered. "Computers are for nerds. Like you, Alotsa Snotsa."

Then he grabbed *my* science project.

"What's this?" he demanded.

"It's a volcano. But it doesn't just shoot stuff out of the top like most science project volcanoes. See? I have it set up so the whole top will explode, which is what real volcanoes do sometimes. And see these little buildings and tiny fake trees down here at the bottom? Those will be swept away and destroyed when—"

"Give that to me," Bryan said.

"What?"

"You heard me. You hand in the stupid computer thing. I'm handing in the volcano. I mean, that's kind of cool. And since I'm a cool guy, I should have it. The computer thing is nerd central, and you're a nerd, so you should turn that in. It makes perfect sense."

What could I say? In a way it did make sense. Kind of.

So, he turned in the volcano. I turned in the computer.

And then the teacher asked him to demonstrate the volcano so the whole class could enjoy it.

"I'll need my assistant, Alonzo," Bryan said smoothly. He had no idea how to make the project work. "It takes two people to operate the Volcano of Doom."

"Certainly," the teacher said.

So we did.

The two of us stood there, side by side. Bryan grinned confidently.

"Go ahead," he whispered to me. Then, in a louder voice everyone could hear, he said, "My assistant, Alonzo, will now begin the volcanic process."

"Okay," I said. "This volcano is made of wire and papier mâché and plain old, everyday dirt."

I pressed the concealed button in the back of the volcano. But when I looked over at Bryan, I saw something disturbing.

There was a wet stain.

A stain that turned Bryan's jeans from stonewashed to indigo blue.

A stain right where you never want a stain to appear.

Dreaded yellow stain!

Bryan had begun to SQUIRT!

Bryan's eyes opened wide.

At the same time, the volcano had begun to bubble up. The chemicals surged toward the top opening.

But this is one thing I was totally sure of: the stain happened *before* the volcano erupted. No question about it.

Bryan clutched at his area. He turned his wild eyes to me, like maybe I could help him.

But what could I do?

"Hey," one of the kids in the front row said. "Bryan's staining!"

"Where?" another kid wondered. He craned his neck to see. Then he laughed. "Hey, Bryan! You're presoaking the fabric!"

The teacher frowned. "Bryan, that is *entirely* inappropriate behavior."

"Hey, Bryan? Is there a fire? Is that why you're trying to put it out?"

And all the while, the stain grew. And GREW!

"It's . . . it's . . . ," Bryan tried desperately to think of some explanation.

But he was way too panicked to think clearly. Not that he was ever exactly a genius.

He clutched his area and squeezed his knees together. But now there was drippage. This fact did not escape the notice of the other kids.

"Puddle!"

"Bryan's making a lake! Lake Whoa-I've-gone!"

"Bryan's got a river going. I think it's the Missippissi!"

"If he keeps going it'll be an ocean. Hey, Bryan, is that the Atlantic or the Pissific?"

These jokes got laughs. Even the teacher kind of snorked a little giggle. Actually, I laughed too. I mean, it was funny.

But Bryan shot me a look that made my throat seize up. He was upset, I think.

Meanwhile the volcano was erupting but absolutely no one cared.

"It's . . . ," Bryan repeated helplessly. "It's . . . it's . . ."

What could I do? I couldn't just let him die of embarrassment. I had to help him out. Didn't I?

"Hey, you guys," I said. "That's *not* squirt. It's the chemicals from the volcano. See? It erupted out of the back all over Bryan's jeans."

Bryan's desperate eyes focused again. "That's right!" he cried.

The kids looked pretty skeptical.

"It's true!" Bryan cried. "It's the stupid volcano! Stupid, stupid volcano! It's . . . it's Alonzo's fault! He *made* the stupid volcano!"

I just stared at him. What was he doing?

Bryan glared at me. "You moron! Your stupid volcano ruined my pants! I'm gonna pound you!"

He jumped at me, hands outstretched. He was actually choking me when Mr. Sandoval pulled him away.

Once again, I had to wonder: was Bryan really all that good a friend?

But more interestingly, I had to wonder what was wrong with Bryan lately. And what did it mean for me?

SEVEN

To wee or not to wee? That is the question.

—Shakespew

"Okay, Alonzo, you read the *girl* part. The part that *Kelly* will be playing," Bryan said. He thrust the script into my hands. "I read whatever says Romeo. You just read whatever says Juliet."

"Okay."

It was the next day, and we were at Bryan's house. He lives right next door.

He has a very cool room, of course. There are posters all over his wall. He has this collection of action figures that he's taken apart and glued back the wrong way. So

45

Spiderman's head is on Godzilla's body and so on.

Plus, he has this little hangman's noose he made, and he has the guy from *Star Trek* hanging there. But that kind of gives me the willies.

"But soft!" Bryan began. "What light through yonder window breaks? It is the east, and Juliet is the sun!"

And he went on and on, all by memory. I mean, it was kind of incredible. Bryan really isn't all that smart, usually, but he could memorize lines. Plus, he could say them like he meant them.

I was so surprised watching him do his lines I almost missed it when it was my turn to talk. All I had to say was "Ay, me!"

So, when Bryan said "O! That I were a glove upon that hand, that I might touch that cheek," I was supposed to say "Ay, me!" But I totally spaced out. "What?" I said.

Bryan glared furiously at me. "You hopeless bag of used toilet paper! Are you a complete idiot? I swear, I am going to pound you into the dirt!"

46

And that is when the stain began to appear. Just a little dark stain about the size of a quarter at first. But it grew quickly.

Very quickly!

"Bryan!" I yelled.

"What?" he demanded. "I'm trying to do this play, moron! Don't keep interrupting!"

"But Bryan . . . look!" I pointed at the stain, which now was about three inches wide.

Bryan looked down. He screamed. "Ahhh-hhhhhhh!"

His screaming scared me. "Ahhhhhhhhh!"

"I'm squirting!" he cried.

"Well, just stop," I said.

"I can't! I can't stop! I CAN'T STOP SQUIRTING!"

I felt a terrible thrill of fear go up and down my spine. I've never seen pure, helpless horror before. Except in the mirror. And it was weird seeing Bryan so afraid.

Weird and . . . well, something else. I wasn't sure what. But it was a sort of *good* feeling. One of those good feelings that makes you feel bad.

"Just stop," I repeated. "You can just STOP."

But the stain was growing. A puddle was forming. It was spreading across the floor of Bryan's bedroom. Several action figures looked as if they might be drowned.

I backed away as the yellow lake edged toward my shoes.

"Don't leave me!" Bryan wailed. "You're supposed to be my friend."

"I'm not leaving," I said. "I'm just . . . getting to higher ground."

"You think this is FUNNY?" Bryan screeched.

Well, actually . . . But I figured it would not be very smart for me to laugh. Besides, my brain was busily working.

Hmmm.

Twice now Bryan had launched out-of-control fartillery barrages. The first time had been just as he was leaving Zaraband's show.

Hmmm.

Twice now he had played drench the denim. All this had occurred *after* going to see Zaraband.

Hmmm.

48

But, wait. He had also had two recent snottal extrusions of a massive nature. Those had happened *before* Zaraband.

Double hmmm.

"You gotta help me!" Bryan wailed. "I can't stop! I can't stop the flow! I'm draining! I'm draining away!"

His panicky voice roused me from my thinking. I suddenly noticed that what had been a piddle puddle was rapidly becoming the Yellow River.

"Look out!" I yelled. "It's heading for the door!"

"No! NO! That's the hallway. My parents will see!"

"You have to stop it!" I said. "Bryan, just turn off the flow!"

"You don't understand. I can't! I can't!"

"We have to stop the stream before it escapes," I said. I grabbed at the first thing I saw. It turned out to be a pillow from Bryan's bed. I raced to the door, just inches ahead of the deadly stream.

I threw the pillow down in the path of the onrushing river.

"What are you doing, you MORON! You IDIOT!" Bryan screamed. "That's my pillow."

He snatched the pillow up from the floor. The whiz rushed beneath the crack of the door.

"Oh no! *Now* look what you've done!" Bryan yelled. "Alonzo! You let it get out in the hallway!"

He threw open the door and rushed out into the hall. I rushed after him.

We stopped and stared in utter horror.

The stairs!

"No!" Bryan cried. "No! It's gonna go Niagara!"

But it was too late. Nothing could stop the whizzerfall as it flowed down the stairs, leaping and burbling from one step to the next.

Later, Bryan's parents came home. He blamed it all on me. It was only natural, I guess. I mean, he was pretty embarrassed.

His parents told me I should see a doctor. And in the meantime they'd really prefer if I didn't come over.

EIGHT

Once more blow out the breach, dear friend, once more!

—Shakespew

That night as I lay in bed I went over it all in my mind. I tried to recall each incident.

I was all ready to conclude that Zaraband was responsible somehow. But how about the two major snotters? Those had happened *before* Zaraband.

Then, it suddenly hit me: Bryan was scared and embarrassed by the two fart attacks and the two unexpected rain showers.

But he had *not* been upset about the nose pudding.

"Aha!" I cried. I sat up in my bed and snapped on the light. So, the snotters were different. Those were just Bryan being funny. The other things . . . those were Zaraband's doing.

Trigger words. Wasn't that what Zaraband had called them? He had hypnotized Bryan and implanted trigger words to make him fart and squirt!

It was diabolical! It was cruel! It was not even slightly nice!

But what *were* the words? I had to remember. I had to know.

Earlier, when we had been practicing for the play, what was the last thing either of us had said? The last word before . . .

It came to me in a flash. Bryan had said "I'll pound you into the dirt!"

Dirt? Was *dirt* the trigger word for squirt?

Yes! That was it! The other day, while we were demonstrating the volcano, I had mentioned that it was made of wire, papier mâché, and *dirt!*

It was easier to figure out the word that triggered farting. I recalled clearly that as we left the theater, Zaraband had said "Depart." The same word Kelly had used just before

Bryan began firing poppers on the bus.

I nodded in satisfaction and turned off the light.

"Depart" and "dirt." I was pretty sure about it. Those were the trigger words.

But how could I be positive?

I got up from my bed. My parents were still awake watching TV downstairs, so I was very quiet. I went to the phone in our upstairs hallway and carried it to my room.

I sat by my window in the dark. It's only about fifty feet to Bryan's house. His window is easy to spot. The light was still on over there.

I dialed Bryan's number.

"Hello?"

It was his dad. I made a snap decision to change my voice. I made it sound as low as I could. "Hello? May I speak to Bryan?"

"Who is this? Is this Alonzo?"

"No, sir. This is . . . um . . . Tony. It's important for me to speak to Bryan."

"Okay," he said doubtfully.

Then I heard him yell, "Bryan! Telephone! And whoever it is, tell them not to call you so late!"

I waited nervously. I actually chewed my fingernails.

Through the window I could see Bryan walking to the phone. He has his own extension in his room. He was wearing pajama bottoms and a T-shirt.

Bryan picked up the receiver. "Yeah? Who is it?"

I took a deep breath to steady the quivering in my stomach. "Depart," I said. Then I hung up the phone.

For several seconds, nothing happened.

Bryan just stood there, staring at the phone like he couldn't believe some idiot was calling him to say one stupid word.

Then . . .

Ka-BOOOOOOOOOOOOOOOOOM!

Shatter!

Crash!

The glass in Bryan's bedroom window exploded outward. It was blown into a thousand pieces!

Then . . . no, it is too bizarre, too incredible. You'll never believe me. You'll think I'm making it up.

But it's true. True, I tell you!

Bryan flew.

He flew through the window like a cannonball.

He flew through the air!

His arms and legs were bowed back by the mighty force of the fart blast.

Face first he launched through the blown-out window!

I'm telling you, I SAW him fly like a rocket.

"Aaaaaaaahhhhhhhh!" Bryan screamed as he flew through the air.

Flump!

"Owww!"

I pressed my nose against the glass, straining to see if he had survived. But I kept my light off so he couldn't see me.

He seemed shaken, but not injured. Mostly, he looked scared. Very scared.

But then, who wouldn't be? Not only was he under the control of Zaraband's trigger words—each attack was worse than the one before.

One more "dirt" and Bryan might pee till he was completely drained away!

One more "depart" and the awful force of

the supernatural farts might kill him! And if the explosion didn't, the stench would.

I crawled back in my bed and pulled the covers over my head. The next day I would go to Zaraband. I would find a way to save Bryan.

Bryan would be really grateful if I saved him. Grateful . . . Bryan . . .

Yes, it was hard to picture him being grateful. More likely he would noogie me till my head was raw and blame me for everything.

"Well, if he does that," I muttered, "I could just say 'depart.' Or 'dirt.'"

Instantly I felt ashamed. But at the same time, I laughed a little.

"Heh heh heh."

It was a rotten thing to even *think*. I scolded myself for being so mean. After all, despite everything, Bryan was my friend.

"Heh heh heh."

No, really. It would be wrong to use this power to control Bryan.

Totally, totally wrong.

"Heh heh heh."

NINE

I am a man more barfed upon than barfing.
—Shakespew

The next day after school I snuck away fast before Bryan could notice me. Not that he had said much to me all day. He seemed like maybe he was a little shaken up.

I guess it's a pretty shocking experience to fart-blast yourself clear out the window.

"Heh heh heh."

Stop that! I ordered myself firmly. For some reason I had been laughing a lot since the day before.

But it was wrong. Bryan was my friend. And he was hurting.

"Heh heh heh."

Today was the first day of rehearsal for Romeo and Juliet. Today he might even have to kiss Kelly Armstrong. Unless she happened to say "depart" again. Or "dirt."

"Heh heh heh."

I hopped a city bus straight from school and headed downtown. I got off right across the street from the theater of Zaraband the Magnificent.

The ticket lady said they were between shows. Zaraband was back in his dressing room. But she wouldn't let me in.

So I snuck around behind the theater and found a stage door. Zaraband was standing there. He was smoking a big cigar. I guess it was a No Smoking theater.

"Hello, Mr. Zaraband?" I said.

He gave me a totally disinterested look. "Whaddya want, kid?"

"Um, maybe you don't remember me. I was at your show with a friend of mine a few days ago."

"Look, if you want your money back, the answer's no. Now beat it." He took a long puff on his cigar. Then he started coughing.

I waited till he was done coughing. It was quite a while. Then I said, "I was there with a friend of mine named Bryan. You did something to him. I guess he was being kind of rude."

Zaraband's eyes lit up. "Oh yeah. I remember now. The brat. How's he like his life now, the little monster?"

I gulped. Obviously Zaraband was not a very forgiving person. "I finally figured it out. I mean, anytime someone says 'dirt' Bryan has to squirt. And if anyone says 'depart' he has to fart."

"Pretty good, eh?" Zaraband said. Then he laughed. Then he coughed some more.

"He squirted in front of the whole class."

"Hee hee hee!" Zaraband giggled. "Excellent! Perfect!"

"Look, sir, you don't understand. Each time he does it, it gets worse! Last night he fart-launched. He blew a major rocket-toot. He went totally *airborne!*"

Zaraband stopped laughing instantly. The cigar dropped from his shocked fingers. And

I didn't even know fingers could experience emotions!

"What?" Zaraband snapped. "You're telling me that each time he dribbles or fires off a popper, it gets worse?"

"Yes, sir. Much worse. I'm afraid one more 'depart' may kill him!"

Zaraband looked very worried. "This is bad," he said. "It's the multiplier effect. It's . . . it's beyond regular hypnosis. This is a supernatural occurrence. It happens only in very rare cases. Some greater power must have it in for your friend Bryan. Either that or it's because I got pushy and added the gasser effect to the five regrettables. Oh, why? Why did I try to add the farts?"

"What can I do to help Bryan?" I asked.

Zaraband shrugged. He bent over and fished his cigar up off the ground. "Okay, here's the deal, kid. I based my trigger words on the five regrettable fluids." He looked suspiciously at me. "You know about the five regrettable fluids?"

I shook my head.

"It's a very ancient teaching. It goes back to

the dark ages. The five regrettable fluids are: pukus, mucus, waximus auriculus, numero uno, and numero dos. But that's Latin. I don't suppose you understand, schools today being the way they are. Translated, the five regrettable fluids are heave, boogers, ear wax, squirt, and buttwurst. I threw in the farts as an extra. Your friend got on my nerves, the little . . . anyway, that must be what went wrong: Never add or subtract to the five regrettables. I should *not* have added the fart trigger."

He bit his lip in a show of regret.

I nodded up at him. I felt honored. He was obviously a very educated person. And I take every opportunity to further my education.

"Anyway," Zaraband said, "I used one trigger word for each of the five regrettables plus a sixth word for the gasser. 'Depart' for fart. 'Dirt' for squirt. 'Tax' for ear wax. 'Plot' for snot. 'Comet' for vomit. And, of course, 'droop.'"

I made a mental note of each word. I knew I would need to rememember them later. "But how can I stop—"

"Wait. There's one *more* word you need to know. It is the most dangerous of all. That word is 'wherefore.'"

"What for?"

"No, '*wherefore.*' It's a word you never hear anyone say. Which is a good thing."

I felt a slow, creeping sense of horror. "O Romeo, Romeo, wherefore art thou Romeo!" I recited.

"Yeah, like that," Zaraband said. "When your friend hears someone say 'wherefore' he will produce a megawad—the deadly combination of all five regrettable fluids at once. He will fire all of his guns at once, so to speak."

"No!" I gasped. "No!"

The rehearsal!

This . . . this was monstrous!

One "wherefore" and Bryan would extrude all five regrettable fluids at once and form the dreaded megwad!

I started to run for the bus.

"Hey, wait!" Zaraband yelled after me. "You need the master word. It's the Latin word for 'regrettable,' which is 'bummerus

62

maximus.' Just say 'bummerus maximus' and your friend will no longer be under my hypnotic spell."

"Thanks!" I yelled back to him.

"Hey, kid. One other thing. If you ever want to put the spell back *on*, just say it twice. 'Bummerus maximus' once and the spell goes away. Twice and it comes back."

I kind of nodded. But I was mystified. Why would I ever need to put the spell back on?

"Heh heh heh."

TEN

Blow, blow, thou buttal wind, thou art not so un-kind as man's ingratitude.

—Shakespew

I ran for the bus. But it pulled away just as I got there.

"Noooooooo!" I cried.

"There's another bus in twenty minutes," a lady said.

"Noooooooo! That's too long."

I took off at a run. I had to reach Bryan before Kelly said the deadly word "wherefore."

And I was pretty sure they would be practicing that part of the play today.

Kelly would say, "Romeo, Romeo, where-fore—" and Bryan would virtually explode in a massive assault of all five regrettable fluids with supplemental fartillery!

"Heh heh heh."

NO! No "heh heh heh!" Kelly would be there. She could be killed!

It was about two miles from downtown to the school.

I ran.

I stumbled.

I staggered.

I leaped over dividers and crawled through fences. Bushes and brambles whipped at my face and hands. Leaves and branches tangled my arms. I saw the signs of falling rocks, animal crossings, and toll roads!

I was gasping and panting, and I was ready to collapse by the time I reached the school.

Was I too late? Had Kelly already said the deadly "wherefore"? Had Bryan farted and gooed himself into oblivion?

I staggered, exhausted, to the auditorium.

I threw open the door.

I stared at the stage. Bryan and Kelly were

there. Mr. Stipe was standing nearby.

Bryan was saying, "O! Speak again bright angel; for thou art as glorious to this night, being o'er my head as a winged messenger of heaven . . ."

I knew the passage! There were exactly four more lines. Then . . .

"Stop!" I yelled. But I was so worn out that my voice was weak. They couldn't hear me at the front of the auditorium.

Bryan was still talking! And I could see Kelly getting ready to fire the fateful "wherefore"!

I raced with my last remaining strength down the aisle.

"When he bestrides the lazy-pacing clouds and sails upon—"

I wasn't going to make it! All Bryan had to say was "the bosom of the air!"

I dug deep and found my last ounce of strength. I hurled myself upon the stage. I had to say the master words! I had to free Bryan from Zaraband's spell. If I could just say it!

"Bumm . . ." Gasp. ". . . bummer . . ." Pant.

I swallowed hard and said, "Bummerus maximus!"

I collapsed. My work was done. I had saved my friend. And innocent bystanders too.

I was a hero.

Me, Alonzo, a hero!

Bryan came and stood over me.

He looked down at me and shook his head.

"This is so pathetic, you moron, dweeb, loser, fart knocker," he said.

"But . . . but . . . but Bryan!"

Bryan smirked at Kelly. "You know why he's being such a squirrel?" Bryan asked her. "Because he's in looooove with you, that's why. He wanted to get this part so he could kissy kissy kissy you."

I was horrified!

Kelly . . . beautiful, angelic Kelly was looking at me with an expression of either utter contempt or vague amusement, and I was betting on contempt.

Then Bryan kicked me. It wasn't a hard kick. Just a little kick. But it meant a lot.

"I've had it with you, loser worm boy," he said to me. "Get out of here and don't waste my time ever again."

Then he laughed. He *laughed!* And turned to Kelly and said, "See what happens when you try to be nice to losers? They just end up embarrassing you."

I was stunned. I was horrified. I have never felt so low.

I had saved Bryan. He had repaid me by humiliating me in front of the one person I cared about: Kelly Armstrong!

ELEVEN

Friends, Romans, Countrymen, lend me your ear wax.

—Shakespew

That evening I sat in my room and realized the awful truth—my entire life had been a lie.

Okay, not my *entire* life. But certainly my friendship with Bryan.

I realized now—he wasn't really my friend after all. All that bullying I'd put up with was just bullying. It wasn't friendly teasing, it was bullying!

The fog had lifted.

The scales had fallen from my eyes!

Whatever that means.

I could see what Bryan really was: a JERK!

And I could see what I really was too: a WIENER!

A wuss, a patsy, a wimp, a weakling, a baby, a whipping boy, a victim, a toady, a bootlick, a brownnoser, a suck-up.

I was a future guest on Sally Jessy Raphael! Yes, *that's* how low I was.

"Noooooooooo!" I wailed.

"Honey? Are you okay?" My mom asked. She was passing by my room.

"Yes, mom, I'm fine. I just realized I've been a loser for years and years. I've been a kiss-up, a pansy, a spineless worm, a—"

"As long as you're okay, dear," my mom said.

I buried my head in my pillows and sobbed uncontrollably. I boo-hooed for an hour or so, then stopped to watch *Friends*. Then I boo-hooed some more.

At last, I was out of tears.

I raised my tear-stained face from my pillows. I stood up. I looked at myself in the mirror.

"No more!" I said.

Suddenly, I was seized by a powerful anger. It was a rage. Yes, more of a rage than just an ordinary anger. And I was seized by it.

"NO MORE!" I cried and shook my fist. "I'm mad as heck and I won't take it anymore! I'll get him. I'll pay him back for every humiliation. I'll make him regret every time he made me do his homework. He'll rue the day he noogied me!"

But how to . . . oh. Oh!

"Heh heh heh."

But of course. It would be so easy. It would be so terrible. It would be the end of Bryan the Bully.

"Nyah hah hah hah HAH!" I laughed, with a mad gleam in my eye.

"The play! The PLAY! The play's the thing!"

Bummerus maximus, the Latin words meaning "regrettable." Those are what I needed. The magic words. If I said it twice, Bryan would be back under Zaraband's spell. If I said it once, the spell ended again.

It was a switch. I could turn Bryan on and off like a light.

The next day was Friday. The play was Saturday. That would be when I would strike the final blow. But in the meantime, I could have a little fun.

The next morning I saw Bryan at the bus stop, as usual. But nothing was as usual anymore.

"Stay away from me, loser," he said. "I'm done with you, Alotsa Snotsa."

"Okay, Bryan. I just wanted to say . . . bummerus maximus, bummerus maximus."

"What?"

I grinned. I had just renewed Zaraband's hypnotic spell. "Nothing, Bryan. Nothing at all. Heh heh heh."

I waited till lunch. I thought lunch would be a good time to launch my first attack. I had put a lot of thought into which trigger word to use first.

I had settled on the strangest and rarest of the five regrettable fluids: waximus auriculus. Ear wax. The trigger word according to Zaraband was "tax."

Bryan loaded up his tray as usual. And when he passed by me he reached over and grabbed my Hostess cupcake without even saying a word. Then he went and sat at a table with Kelly.

Kelly kind of rolled her eyes when he sat down with her. But I knew she would be rolling more than her eyes soon.

I was fired up. I was ready. The worm was turning. I could practically feel a spine growing inside me.

I walked right behind Bryan and said, "Hi, Kelly. I hope you won't let Bryan . . . *tax* . . . your patience." Then, just for good measure, I said, "Tax!" again, nice and loud.

At first nothing happened. Bryan just turned around and glared like he was going to get up and pound me.

But then it began.

I noticed a thin stream of orange goo dribbling out of his ears. It filled his ear holes, then spilled out and down the side of his face.

I grinned. "Hey, Bryan," I said. "That's kind of gross."

"What?" he demanded. "You calling *me* gross, fart sniffer?"

By then the thin trickle of orange substance had speeded up. Two creamsicle-colored streams were dribbling down Bryan's cheeks, heading toward a meeting at his chin.

"Ewwwwwww!" Kelly's friend Jenny said. She pointed at Bryan and covered her mouth with her hand.

"Oh, guh-ROSS!" someone cried out.

"Look! Look at Bryan's ears! I've never seen anything like it!"

It was definitely weird. I mean, I never knew how much ear wax the average head contains. But judging from Bryan it looks like maybe most of what you *think* is your brain is actually orange substance.

Bryan reached up and wiped at his ears. His hand came away covered with a smear the color of Chee•tos.

"AAAARRRGGGHHH!"

He looked at me in total horror. He spun around in panic, looking left and right for help. Droplets of ear wax flew through the air.

A big one landed on Kelly's forehead.

SPLAT! Like a big, orange raindrop.

"EWWWWWWW! Guh-ROSS! GROSS! GROSS!"

Kelly wiped the deadly stain away, but now it was on her hand!

"That's about enough, for now," I muttered under my breath. "More later."

I grinned at Bryan and said, "Bummerus maximus, Bryan."

He was too crazed even to hear me—consciously. But his unconscious heard. And the waxy goo stopped flowing.

But he was still yelling "Aaaaarrrrggghhh!" as he wiped helplessly at the ear dribble.

I had switched off the spell. For now. I didn't want anyone else accidentally setting him off.

Oh no. He was mine. All mine.

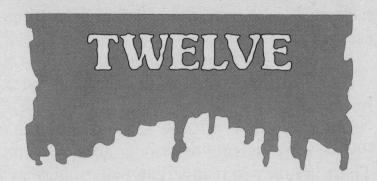

TWELVE

What's in a name? That which we call vomit or gumbo or puke or stomach contents or heave or hurl, by any other name would smell as morbific.

—Shakespew

"Depart" for fart. "Dirt" for squirt. "Tax" for ear wax. "Plot" for snot. "Comet" for vomit. And "droop" for poop.

And of course, "wherefore."

The words of power. Total power!

I had absolute control over Bryan.

Absolute control. The worm had turned. The wuss was in charge now.

"Heh heh heh."

On the bus home at the end of the day

Bryan glared suspiciously at me. I think he suspected I was responsible for his disgusting ear wax production.

He just didn't know *how*.

As he sat there, he kept checking his ears. Just in case.

I noticed that no one sat next to him. People were starting to wonder about Bryan. There are only so many times you can display supernaturally disgusting behavior before other kids will start to wonder about you.

I decided the time had come to end all doubts about Bryan. It was time for . . . the comet.

"Heh heh heh."

There was just one problem. Bryan was sitting in the middle of the bus. Kelly was just one row ahead of him. She would be in terrible danger.

But then again, problems are really opportunities.

"Heh heh heh."

I would save her when Bryan began to respond to the trigger word. That's what I had to do.

I got up and wobbled my way down the aisle as if I were heading to the back of the bus. As I passed Bryan I said, in a whisper that only he could hear, "Bummerus maximus, bummerus maximus."

He gave me an angry glare. "You said that before. Am I supposed to be impressed because you speak Latin? Latin's a dead language."

I just walked on by. I went to the back of the bus. Then I turned around.

I took a deep breath. Bryan was just a few rows ahead of me now. And Kelly was just in front of him. This would require courage and lightning fast reflexes on my part.

Three more steps. Two. One.

"COMET!"

I leapt. I grabbed Kelly's arm. I yanked her out of her seat.

"What are you—" she began to protest. But then she heard Bryan.

"Guh guh guh . . . ," Bryan said.

He had started to sing the vocals of vomit.

Kelly is very smart. She immediately saw what was happening. "He's doing the gack dance!" she cried. "Bryan's gonna heave!"

"Gack dance!" a girl screamed.

"Nobody chucks on the bus!" the bus driver cried. But it was too late.

"Look out! Bryan's doing the blew magoo!"

"Guh guh GOV-BLEEEEAAAAAHH-HHH!"

Bryan launched his lunch. I dragged Kelly to the front of the bus, but even there we were not safe.

"Gug gug BLEAAAAAAAH BLEEEAA-AAAHH! GovBLEEEEAAAAAHHHH!"

I had underestimated! I had expected a Force 6 Barficane—a basic barf. Maybe a Force 7, a true puke storm. But Bryan had gone fire hose!

I had unleashed a Force 8! What had I *done?*

Stomach contents emitted at fire hose intensity! Bryan tried to clam his jaw down but the force of the guttal explosion blew out a tooth!

"Help! Help! I'm magoooooooooooed!" a little girl screamed.

The gumbo stream began to claim casualties.

SPLATTTTT!

A girl with black hair and glasses was hit in the back of the head and knocked from her seat.

BAH-LOOOOSHH!

A guy trying to run away was hit by the guttal explosion. He screamed. "Aiiiieeeee!" and was thrown through the air and landed in a crumpled heap.

Bryan's eyes were wide with terror. He looked right at Kelly. His aim followed his eyes.

I stepped in front of Kelly. I could not let her be magooed! This was between me and Bryan. And, okay, a few dozen innocent bystanders.

Bryan stood up, wild with panic. That was his big mistake. He was safer sitting down.

"GOV-BLLEEEEEAAAAAHHHHH!"

He hurled. But without the seat back to stop him, Bryan had no choice but to obey the laws of thermodynamics. For every action there is an equal and opposite reaction.

The Force 8 vomitation exploded from his mouth.

Shoooooooom!

It blew him off his feet! He flipped back, landed on his butt, and shot like a hockey puck toward the back door of the bus.

Fortunately, the bus driver had pulled over.

CRASH! Bryan blew through the back door, propelled by his own barf stream.

He landed on the road behind the bus. Alive, unhurt, but minus a tooth and several organs.

I turned to look at Kelly. Yes! Kelly was safe!

"You . . . Alonzo, you saved me!" she said.

I blushed. "It was nothing."

"But I was right in the seat in front of him. I . . . I could have been utterly gumboed. I will never forget what you did for me," she said.

And then she took my hand in hers and gave it a warm, friendly squeeze of gratitude.

My life was definitely turning around.

THIRTEEN

Cry havoc! And let slip the regrettable fluids of war!

—Shakespew

After the horrible destruction on the bus, I almost felt bad for Bryan. I mean, it was hard for me to totally stop thinking of him as a friend.

Then, something kind of miraculous happened.

I was in the living room, watching TV. The doorbell rang. My mom answered it.

"Alonzo? It's for you. Someone named Kelly."

I practically flew off the couch. I raced for the front door.

She stood there, bathed in the radiant glow of the porch light. Moths circled her head like . . . um, like . . . like something nice.

"K-K-Kelly?" I stammered.

She put her hands on her hips and gave me a very direct look. "I have to ask you a question, Alonzo."

"Me? You have to ask *me* a question?"

"Yes. You know, I thought you were a real gentleman today when you saved me from being vomitized. But . . . well, I just got a call from Bryan. I guess you know he's playing Romeo with me."

Yes, I knew. And it ate away at me like a worm in my guts!

"Uh-huh," I said.

"Well, Bryan says the reason he heaved was that you poisoned him."

"Excuse me?"

"Bryan says you deliberately poisoned him because you were jealous over *him* being in the play with *me*."

I just stood there with my mouth open for a few minutes. I could not believe what I was hearing. Me? Poison Bryan?

"Kelly, of course that is totally *not* true." I said.

"I didn't think it was," she said. She sighed. "I mean, I know Bryan is a bully. And I've watched the way he treats you."

I gulped. "You have?"

"Yes. I guess . . . I mean, I guess I thought you were interesting. So I kind of noticed you sometimes. And whenever I would see you two together, Bryan would be doing something rotten to you." Suddenly her voice changed. It became hard and angry. "I can't stand bullies. I really hate people like that."

"You do?"

"Yes. See, I used to be bothered by a bully. It was a few years ago. This horrible girl named Andrea. She used to pick on me all the time. Till finally, she stopped."

"What made her stop?" I asked. This was a whole new angle on Kelly. I hadn't even realized there was such a thing as a girl bully.

"She stopped after I locked her in her own gym locker with her own smelly gym clothes. And some bees. Since then she's been very pleasant."

I really didn't want to think too much about that. "So . . . you think revenge is okay?"

Kelly smiled. It was a different smile than I'd ever seen on her before. It wasn't the smile of an angel like it usually was.

"Bullies deserve no mercy," Kelly said. She clenched her fist and got a wild look in her beautiful blue eyes. "NO mercy! What I came to tell you was, if you *had* poisoned Bryan so he gacked up his kidneys, that would have been okay by me. I would have just laughed! *Laughed!* Nyah hah hah hah!"

I nodded. I felt as though I had grown close to Kelly in just the few moments we had spent on the porch.

I also felt as if maybe it wasn't all that bad, my not being Romeo. It seemed to me like maybe Kelly was better from a distance. You know?

But I didn't tell *her* that. I just backed away a step or two and said, "Look, Kelly? At the play tomorrow night? Don't wear any good shoes. It's just possible they might get messed up."

Then Kelly asked if I would like to hang out with her. But I told her I had a lot of homework to do.

I said goodnight, and closed the door.

So. Bryan was *still* trying to blame everything on me. Well, he deserved what was coming to him.

And what was coming to him would be most regrettable.

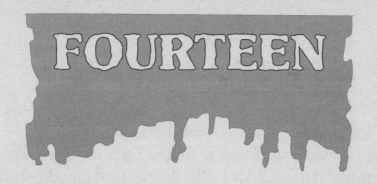

FOURTEEN

But be not afraid of grossness: some men are born gross, some achieve grossness, and some have grossness thrust upon them.

—Shakespew

The play was kind of a big deal. I mean, not just students were there. A lot of parents were there too. The auditorium was jammed with people. There were even some people standing at the back of the room against the walls.

I guess there isn't much to do on a Saturday night in our town.

I went to the play that night looking for revenge. But I am such a nice person I still wanted to give Bryan one more chance.

"Heh heh heh."

No, really. I really did want to give him one more chance.

"Heh heh heh."

While the last people were still filing in, looking for seats, I went backstage.

It was frantic back there. Lots of kids running around. And Mr. Stipe looked like he was losing his mind.

"What do you *mean* Arthur has the trots? He can't be sick. He's our Benvolio! We can't have Romeo and Juliet without Benvolio!"

I ignored him and went looking for Bryan. I found him getting into his costume and playing with his costume sword.

"What are you doing here, loser?" he demanded when he saw me.

I shrugged. "I just came to wish you luck."

He made a face. "Who asked you? Get out of here. I have to get ready."

I didn't leave. "Bryan, I thought we were friends, man."

He laughed. "Friends? Me and a creep like you? I don't think so."

Still I didn't leave. See, I wanted to give him every possible chance to be a decent human being.

"Kelly told me you said I poisoned you."

"Yeah? So what?"

"So, it isn't true."

"I say it *is*." He moved closer and hunched his shoulders up to look even bigger. "You gonna try and argue with me, worm boy?"

I shook my head regretfully. "You know, Bryan, I can't believe what a jerk you are."

He looked shocked. Also angry. "You calling me a jerk?" he demanded. "*You?* Alotsa Snotsa?"

Suddenly, before I could get away, he grabbed me around the neck. He squeezed tight and started to noogie me viciously.

"Ahhhhh!" I cried.

"I ought to *pound* you!"

"Let me go! Let me go!" I yelled.

Just then, Mr. Stipe appeared. "You two quit horsing around. We have no Benvolio! Romeo's best friend is missing! We have no Benvolio!"

Like a bolt from the blue—sudden inspiration!

"Heh heh heh," I muttered under my breath. Then I said, "Mr. Stipe? I've been running lines with Bryan. I know the part of Benvolio."

"Yes!" Mr. Stipe grabbed me by the shoulders. "Yes! Thank you! Get into costume! We're on in five minutes."

When he was gone I turned to Bryan. "You have noogied your last, Bryan."

"Oh yeah? Who's gonna stop me? You?"

"Yes. Me. With a little help from Zaraband."

"Zaraband? What's he got to do with anything?" Bryan demanded suspiciously.

For once I was the one who got to smirk. "You big moron, Bryan. Why do you think you've been having explosive farts and sudden ear wax extrusions? Not to mention a Force 8 barficane?"

"I've been a little sick," he said doubtfully. "Maybe it was something I ate."

"Wrong! Zaraband hypnotized you with trigger words. Trigger words that control all your bodily functions! Trigger words that I know and control! HAH, Bryan! HAH! Enjoy the play."

Even right then if Bryan had just had the sense to say something nice . . . to apologize . . . whatever . . . he might have been saved.

Maybe.

But, no. Bryan was still Bryan.

"You little wuss, you wouldn't *dare*," he said. "I'd pound you into a stain."

I just smiled at him.

I had done my best.

"Hey, Brian? Bummerus maximus, fart knocker. Bummerus maximus."

And now, I thought, let the play begin.

FIFTEEN

All the world's a stage, and all the guys and girls merely vomiteers.

—Shakespew

The stage lights were bright. The stares of hundreds of people were intimidating. The tights I had to wear were droopy.

But I wasn't going to let any of that stop me. I was on a mission. I was going to bring down a bully.

It was payback time.

But as much as I wanted to get Bryan, I knew I would have to switch off the spell before he reached the big "wherefore" scene.

I mean, the megawad of all five regrettable

97

fluids is not something you mess around with. It's just too dangerous.

Especially when it is combined with near deadly farts.

I mean, I was mad at Bryan. But I wasn't insane!

Offstage Mr. Stipe gave me a nod. It was time. So I said Benvolio's line. "Good morrow, cousin."

And Bryan said Romeo's line. "Is the day so young?"

"But new struck nine."

"Was that my father that went hence so fast?"

It was time to rewrite Shakespeare just a little. I considered the different trigger words. What would be a good way to start?

And then I remembered all the times Bryan had called me Alotsa Snotsa.

Well, it was time see who really was Alotsa Snotsa.

"Yes, it was your father," I said to Bryan as Romeo. "He said something about not liking the . . . *plot!*"

"You toe-jam sucker!" Bryan yelled. "That's not in the play!"

SNORK!

Bryan froze. A wad of pistachio pudding the size of a golf ball had exploded from his nose.

It lay there quivering and glistening on his lip as it slid down toward his mouth.

It looked as if it were alive! It moved!

Bryan quickly grabbed his cape and wiped it off.

He tried to say his next line, which was something like, "Not having that, which having, makes them short."

But he only got as far as "not hav—" before the true nose gusher started to flow.

"Oh, look!" a woman in the audience cried. "That boy! The one who's playing Romeo. He's got a runny nose."

"Runny nose?" another woman said. "That's not just a runny nose. The boy is a snot factory!"

Boogers were flowing from Bryan's nose like runny oatmeal.

"My nose!" Bryan cried. He wiped and wiped but it was like trying to hold back a flood with nothing but a roll of paper towels.

I mean, the guy was snorking nose noodles the size of pythons!

"You," he said, glaring at me. "This is *your* fault!"

Without warning he started coming toward me. His hands were out like he was going to choke me.

But I wasn't worried.

"Hey, Romeo," I said. "*Tax*."

He took two more steps, and for a second I was afraid the trigger word wasn't working.

But then . . . it began. The incredible, impossible, almost supernatural extrusion of the orange substance!

It was like some horrible science fiction horror movie.

Bryan's head was gushing two substances at once! Two of the regrettable fluids simultaneously. He was not only Alotsa Snotsa. He was also Wax to the Max!

Combined green and orange dribbled, then poured, then gushed from four of the five holes in his head.

"*What's happening to meeeeeee?*" he cried.

"Bring down the curtain!" Mr. Stipe yelled from offstage.

"Oh, oh, oh! I'm gonna hurl!" someone in the audience said. Possibly our guidance counselor. "It's . . . too gross! Too gross! Make it STOP!"

Naturally, while all the older people were busy panicking and being grossed out, the kids in the audience were just laughing.

"Hey! Look! Bryan's blowing his brains out!"

"Hey, Bryan. You need to think earth tones, man. Green and orange are *not* your colors."

"Is that nacho cheese I see coming out of your ears? Where are the chips?"

Bryan was not laughing. He was twitching. He was a can of soda that had been shaken up on a hot summer day. The boy was ready to explode.

He started to scream. At me. Which was a mistake for two reasons: one, I had total power over him, and you shouldn't scream at people who have total power over you. And two, whenever he opened his mouth . . . well, let's just say the nose noodles had become a whole waterfall of fettucine al snotto.

"I'm (blub blub) gonna kill (blub gag blub) YOU!" he screamed at me. "Do you (blub, pleah, gag) hear me? I'm (blub, glub, gugh, phoo, blub) gonna KILL YOU!"

"Bring down the curtain you fool!" Mr. Stipe yelled at the top of his lungs.

And quite suddenly, as the crowd gasped and made noises of disgust, the curtain dropped.

And Bryan, snot and ear cheddar flying everywhere as he shook his head in rage, leaped at me!

SIXTEEN

There are more regrettable substances in heaven and in earth than are dreamt of in your philosophy.

—Shakespew

Bryan flew at me!

I tried to back away. But he was too quick.

His arm was around my neck. But I had a feeling this would not be just another noogie. No, I had a feeling he might be slightly angry.

"I'm gonna KILL you!" he screamed.

Which was one clue that he was really angry.

"You're DEAD MEAT, Alonzo!"

He began to choke me. Mr. Stipe rushed

out onstage to save me, but he wasn't strong enough to pry Bryan's fingers from my throat.

I was beginning to see stars. And worst of all, I couldn't even speak. I could not say any of the trigger words!

Then Kelly came rushing out onstage.

"What are you doing, Bryan? Let him go! You're ruining the whole play!"

By this time I was starting to lose consciousness. It seemed a shame, to die onstage.

"Owwwww!" I heard Bryan yelp.

Then . . . suddenly. There was air! Air!

I gasped and choked and breathed in the life-giving air. I looked around and saw that Kelly had pulled Bryan off me by grabbing his ear and twisting it.

Not an easy thing to do since it was coated in orange substance an inch thick.

"Lemme go!" Bryan whined.

Kelly let him go and wiped her hand on his shirt.

"Listen to me, Bryan," she snapped. "This is *my* play. This is my big chance to be onstage. No one is messing it up. Bryan? Get back out there. Alonzo? If you want to ruin Bryan's life it will have to wait."

She put her hands on her hips and glared down at me. "You understand, Alonzo?"

"Urggh . . . urg . . . ," I tried to answer, but I couldn't speak clearly from Bryan choking me. So I just nodded.

"Okay, we're going straight to the big balcony scene," Kelly snapped. "Let's do it!"

Mr. Stipe helped me stagger off the stage.

Bryan's head goos had stopped flowing— for now—and he wiped it all off on a series of paper towels, rags, sleeves, and stage curtains.

I sat in the wings, trying to recover my voice. I felt pretty bad. I had allowed my desire for revenge to mess up the whole show. Now Kelly was mad at me. Mr. Stipe was mad at me. And the audience members who were close enough to the front that they got hit by flying wads of the green and orange substances weren't all that happy either.

What had I done?

"Heh heh heh."

And to think that I had even considered

using the deadly "wherefore" trigger word. The word which . . .

I froze.

From the stage I heard Bryan say, "When he bestrides the lazy-pacing clouds, and sails upon—"

No! NO!

I had never turned off the spell! Bryan was still under the control of Zaraband's trigger words! And in less than three seconds, Kelly (as Juliet) would say the dreaded "wherefore"!

I jumped up. I tried to cry out a warning, but my throat would not let me do any more than gurgle.

I ran toward the stage.

Mr. Stipe caught me and dragged me back!

No! NOOOOOO!

Then, as I watched, panic-stricken and horrified, Kelly (as Juliet) said the fatal line.

"O Romeo, Romeo! Wherefore art thou Romeo?"

I . . . I can't describe what happened next. It was too horrible. Too horrible to speak of. No, no, don't try to make me.

Okay, I'll describe it. But just this once.

It began with a whole new serving of nose noodles. They exploded from Bryan's nostrils with such force that they stuck to Kelly's forehead and actually hung there, like a suspension bridge!

The ear wax flow started again, worse than before.

"Ohhhhhh," the audience moaned. "Not again with the head goo."

If only. If only that had been the end of it.

"Hey! Look! He's draining! He's washing his tights in used water!"

It was true. The Missippissi was flowing to the Pissific again.

It was a flood. It was a gusher. It was a wall of yellow stain rolling across the stage like a tidal wave that would annihilate all in its path!

"No!" Bryan gasped. "NO! Stop it! Stop!" Blub glub "Alonzo, save meeeee!"

"Urgh . . . urgh . . . ," I grunted. I still could not talk! I still could not speak the words that would end this abomination!

The megawad was beginning to form. We

were all witnessing its birth.

It was coming! The megawad!

"Alonzo!" Bryan wailed pitiably. "I'm sorry. I'm sorry." Blub phhpahh blub. "Save me, man!"

It was the last thing he was able to say. Because then the gack dance began.

His stomach did the wiggle and warp. His throat seized and spazzed.

"Gack dance!" a man screamed.

"Oh, no," I heard a woman cry. "I know what's happening! Mucus, waximus auriculus, numero uno. And now, pukus! It's . . . it's . . . it's the megawad!"

I was impressed. She was obviously an educated woman.

"Aaaaaaaaaaahhhhhh!" the woman screamed in sheer terror.

"He's gonna launch!"

"Run! Run! He's gonna do the blew magoo!"

"Gug guh GOVVVV-BLEEEEEEAAA-AAAHHHHH!"

Steaming hot gumbo shot with awesome force from Bryan's mouth! It had power. It had volume. It was . . . yes! A Force 10 Barficane!

Stomach contents showered across the audience.

Bryan was blown backward by the terrible blast.

But then, just when you thought it couldn't get any worse . . .

KA-BOOOOOOOMMMMM!

The fart blew the back of Bryan's tights into shreds! They were smoking! Burning tatters of fabric scattered and drifted.

People were knocked out of their seats. There were screams! Cries! And many unhappy expressions!

"NOOOOO!"

"NO, it can't beeeeeee! He seemed like such a quiet boyyyyy!"

"Save us! Save us!"

"Women and children first!"

I'm telling you, it was utter panic. The vomit-drenched, wax-spotted, snot-bedecked, squirt-surfing mob surged toward the exits.

K A - B O O O O O O O O O M M M M ! BLAAAAAAAT! BLAAAAAAT!

The fartillery was firing steadily now.

"Guh guh GOV-BLEEEEEEEAAAAHHH!"

The Force 10 Barficane was showing no signs of weakening.

And that was when the impossible happened. Bryan began to fly. The power of the farts acted together with the power of the puke storm, and Bryan was shooting around the room like a balloon!

SHHWWOOOOOP!

He flew above the crowd like a crazed bumblebee, spraying all the five regrettable fluids at once!

The megawad had begun to form. It was a huge, viscous ball of nauseating stench and viscosity.

Bryan seemed to be in orbit around it. Flying on fart power, lifted up by the intensity of the barficane.

It would have all ended very, very badly.

But just then, at the back of the room, a thin man wearing a black cape (and coughing) raised his hands.

Zaraband!

He stood tall amid the destruction and panic. And in a loud, clear voice, he said, "Bummerus maximus!"

SEVENTEEN

This is a tale told by an idiot, full of sound and fury and gross substances, and signifying nothing.
—Shakespew

Yes, Zaraband had saved us all in the end. He said he had felt a supernatural disturbance and realized that the megawad was forming.

Of course, he's the one who had started the whole hypnosis thing in the first place. So he wasn't exactly a huge hero or anything.

Just the same, attendance at his shows went way up. And eventually he got a regular gig in Las Vegas, at one of the casinos.

A lot of people were hurt that night. Every

ambulance in the city had to be sent. Some of the injuries were minor—simple snotization or minor orange substance poisoning.

Some were more serious. There were a few cases of megawad disease. But with proper diet, exercise, and repeated showers, everyone recovered.

The real scars were psychological. But hey, what can you do about that?

As for Kelly and Bryan and me, well, a lot has changed since that night.

Kelly is still just a little nutty, and still very beautiful. But she's decided she doesn't want to be in any more school plays.

Bryan is still a bully, but he's found a new kid to pick on. And Bryan's popularity has gone down a little since the night when he flew around the auditorium showering everyone with regrettable fluids. Kids are so fickle, and popularity is fleeting.

As for me, well, I've changed the most. I'm no longer picked on by Bryan. Or anyone, really. See, I had Zaraband teach me that thing he does with his hands to hypnotize people. So everyone is very nice to me.

Very nice.

"Heh heh heh."

Yes, a lot has changed. And I'm pretty sure there was a moral to the story. I don't know what it was, but I'll bet there was one.

Okay, let me think . . . Hmmmm . . . a moral. Hmmmm . . . It will come to me . . . a moral . . .

Oh! Got it! Here's the moral: don't play hooky. Because look what happened to us.

Okay, that's a little weak.

Wait, here's another moral: stand up for yourself. Don't let anyone push you around. See, if I had just stood up for myself to begin with, well . . .

Oh never mind.

Forget the moral. Instead, I would like you to watch my hand. Watch my hand as it waves through the air.

Your eyelids are very heavy. Your eyes are beginning to close. . . .

Glossary of Terms

barficane: *noun*. Barficanes are episodes of vomitation. They are scientifically rated according to strength. A Force 1 being the lowest intensity, and the deadly Force 10 being the highest. (For a complete guide to the Barficane Rating System, see Barf-O-Rama #5.)

blew magoo: *noun*. To heave, to vomit, to extrude, to launch, or to hurl. As in "I was so sick I did the blew magoo." The origins of this phrase are lost in the mists of time.

boogaroni: *noun.* A quick, inexpensive, and easy-to-make snot dish that is often given as a consolation prize on game shows.

buttnado: *noun.* A *tor*nado is formed when a cold air front encounters warmer air. A funnel cloud is created, which then attacks mobile homes. A *butt*nado is formed when a person cuts a huge fart. Buttnados show no special fondness for trailers.

fartillery: *noun.* Powerful and destructive farts that occur in barrages. Outlawed by the Treaty of Versailles after the horrors of trench warfare.

fettuccine al snotto: *noun.* Fett-uh-CHEE-nee al SNOT-o. As this dish contains no tomatoes, it may be assumed to be part of the Northern Italian culinary tradition.

five regrettable fluids: The five regrettables, as they are sometimes called, are pukus, mucus, waximus auriculas, numero uno, and numero dos. In less formal terms, they are gumbo, nose butter, ear orange, squirt, and pooptonium. (A more complete explanation of the history of the five regrettables may be found in Barf-O-Rama #4.)

gack dance: *noun*. The characteristic gagging that precedes an episode of hurling.

gumbo: *noun*. Not sure but believed to involve okra.

megawad: *noun*. First theorized by Copernicus, the megawad is the combination of all of the five regrettable fluids.

Missippissi River: *noun*. They call it Middle-aged Man River, the Stepfather of Waters, the Reasonably Big Muddy. It's every bit as good a river as the Mississippi, but it didn't get a lot of free publicity from Mark Twain. The Missippissi runs from Minnelotopis to Dupuque to St. Loogie, cuts way east to

Blowing Green, Cincisnotti, Pittspew, then races across the south, passing through Rawlfeigh, and eventually reaches the sea at Sarasnota, Florida.

mucustroni: *noun.* Similar to boogaroni, but it comes in a can.

nose noodle: *noun.* Should not be over-cooked.

orange substance: *noun.* Waximus auriculus, ear wax, Q-Tip bait, ear cheddar.

Pissific Ocean: *noun.* Originally thought to have been discovered by Balboa, it was actually discovered by Pissarro.

popper: *noun.* A fart that expresses itself in a loud pop. When extended over the course of several seconds, the popper becomes a multipopper.

snot pudding: *noun.* Now available in new kiwi flavor!

squeezer: *noun.* A type of fart characterized by a trumpetlike sound.

squirt: *noun.* Numero uno, number one, used water, wee wee, (or in French, *non non*), drainage.

vocals of vomit: *noun.* The vocals of vomit may take many forms from simple gagging and gurgling, to groaning and gasping, and finally to gushing.

HERE'S A SNEAK PEEK AT

BARF-O-RAMA #7,

SCAB PIE

"Get out of the way! I've got a stomach full of spiders and I need to barf!"

Ukiah was clutching his stomach. "I need a bowl!"

"NO!" I screamed. "NOOOO!"

Too late.

Gagghhh . . . BLEEEAAAAHHH!

Stinking, steaming hot gumbo bubbled and glopped from Ukiah's mouth. It spilled into the big bowl of mashed pumpkin.

"Ewwwwwwww!" Michelle cried.

"Ewwwwwwww!" I agreed.

And then, we saw something more horrible than any normal barfoleum. The barf was . . . MOVING!

Win FREE

DOCTOR DREADFUL M.D. MONSTER DOCTOR

Prizes!

ENTRY FORM

Name: _____

Address: _____

_____

_____

Birthday: _____ / _____ / _____

OFFICIAL RULES

1. No Purchase Necessary. 2. Entry: To enter, hand print name, address, and birth date on the enclosed official entry form or include information on a 3"x 5" card, and mail to Barf-O-Rama/ Dr. Dreadful Sweepstakes, Bantam Doubleday Dell Young Readers Series Marketing, 1540 Broadway, New York, NY, 10036. Each entry must be received in a separate envelope and mailed separately via first class mail. No copies or mechanical reproductions allowed. Not responsible for lost, late, damaged, misdirected, or postage-due mail. Entries must be received by 11/1/96 and become the property of Bantam Doubleday Dell Young Readers. By participating, entrants agree to be bound by these Official Rules.

3. Drawing: A random drawing will be held on or about 11/27/96 from all eligible entries received by Bantam Doubleday Dell whose decisions are final. Winners will be notified by mail. **4. Prizes:** (1) Grand Prize: A complete set of Dr. Dreadful M.D.™ Toys-estimated retail value of $100.00, (30) First Prizes: Dr. Dreadful M.D.™ Monster Medical Center™ or Dr. Dreadful M.D.™ Creepy Clinic™ - estimated retail value $23.99, (45) Second Prizes: Dr. Dreadful M.D.™ Body Wrap™ Set or Dr. Dreadful M.D.™ Drain-A-Vain™ Set - estimated retail value $10.99, (60) Third Prizes: Dr. Dreadful M.D.™ Rude Remedies™ (Heartburn Brew, Tapeworm Tonic, Blister Fixer, or Bug Lotion) - estimated retail value $7.99. **5. General Conditions:** Sweepstakes open to legal U.S. residents 14 years or younger as of date of entry. All prizes will be awarded. All applicable federal, state, and local laws apply. Void where prohibited or restricted. Winners agree that Bantam Doubleday Dell and Tyco Toys, Inc. will have no liability of any injuries, losses or damages resulting from the acceptance, possession, misuse, or use of the prize. Prizes are nontransferable. Tyco reserves the right to substitute prizes of equal or lesser value. One prize per household or address. No prize or cash substitutes. Odds on winning depend on the number of entries received. **6. For Winners List:** Send self addressed stamped envelope by 2/31/97 to Bantam Doubleday Dell Young Readers Series Marketing, 1540 Broadway, New York, NY, 10036.

Dr. Dreadful trademarks and copyrights are the property of Tyco Industries, Inc.